TWO MOONS

VOLUME ONE
THE IRON NOOSE

TWO MOONS

WRITER - JOHN ARCUDI
ARTIST - VALERIO GIANGIORDANO
COLORS - BILL CRABTREE
LETTERS - MICHAEL HEISLER

TWO MOONS, VOL. 1.
First printing. August 2021. Published by Image Comics, Inc. Office of publication: PO BOX 14457, Portland, OR 97293. Contains material originally published in single magazine form as TWO MOONS #1-5. Printed in the USA. For international rights, contact: foreignlicensing@imagecomics.com. ISBN: 978-1-5343-1911-0.

VOLUME 1: "THE IRON NOOSE"

Logo design by **DREW GILL.**
Design & production by **RYAN BREWER.**

PART 1

Unclaimed by the land that bore us,
Lost in the land, we find
The brave have gone before us;
Cowards are left behind.
Then stand to your glasses, steady;
Here's a health to those we prize.
Here's a toast to the dead already,
And here's to the next who dies.

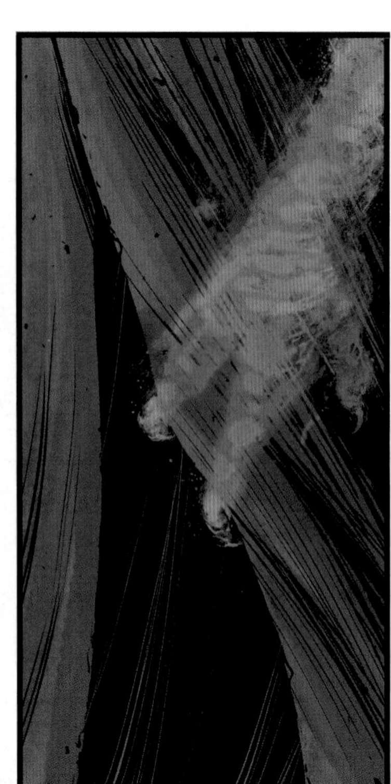

NO!

HEY, VIRGIL! FINALLY GONNA JOIN THE WAR?

HELL, IT'S WELL PAST DAWN, LEVON! WHY DID YOU LET ME SLEEP?
PUT THAT KANSAS TOOTHPICK AWAY. 'LESS YOU PLAN TO SHAVE--IF THAT CHIN O' YOURS EVER SPROUTS.
CORPORAL HATLO!

IS THIS THE MAN WHO IS TO RIDE WITH YOU INTO STERRETT?
YES, MAJOR!

FINE, FINE.
AIN'T BUT THE ONE CASUALTY, BUT WE BE DANGEROUS LOW ON FIELD DRESSINGS. YOU HAUL BACK PLENTY, HEAR?

YES, SERGEANT. MORPHINE, TOO?
ALL 'EY CAN SPARE. A REB PUSH IS COMIN' SOON, CORPORAL.

"AND HELL FOLLOWS WITH 'EM."

BROKEN LEG?
NOT PRECISELY. FOOL SHOT HISSELF ON SENTRY DUTY LAST NIGHT.
VIRGIL, YOU'LL WANNA FETCH THEM BANDAGES.
HOSPITAL
uuuuuhhhhh...
WATER!
NURSE! NURSE!
TWO MOONS.

GRANDFATHER?
HOW DID YOU FIND ME?

BUT WHY? WHY HAVE YOU COME?
YOUR FATHER'S EYES LED ME.
HE STILL WATCHES YOU, BOY.
IRON.
WHAT? WHAT DOES THAT MEAN?
IRON. ONLY IRON.

DID YE KNOW HIM?
!

I FOUND HIM AS I RODE OUT LAST NIGHT. JUST LYING IN THE GRASS LIKE AN ANIMAL.
I BROUGHT HIM BACK BUT THE NIGHT NURSE, SHE'D HAVE NO PART OF HIM, SHE SAID.

SO *I* SAT WITH HIM.
I MADE HIM COMFORTABLE AND SAT WITH HIM UNTIL HE PASSED.

UNTIL HE PASSED?
SOMETHIN' AILS YE?
JUST TIRED, I BELIEVE. BEEN SO LONG SINCE...

YE DO KNOW HIM? HIS PEOPLE WOULD LIKE TO HAVE HIM PROPER BURIED, I'M SURE.
I DON'T KNOW HIM. YOU SHOULD BURY HIM HERE--IF THE TOWN CEMETERY ALLOWS INDIANS.
BUT YE'LL BE WANTIN' THE BANDAGES.
I WISH IT COULD BE MORE, BUT IT'S THE RAIDS UP IN WILMORE. CIVILIAN CASUALTIES IS WHAT I'M MEANIN'.
THOUGH THE FIGHTIN' MEN ARE WORSE STILL. THE THINGS I'VE SEEN THIS LAST WEEK!
MORTAL WOUNDS FILLED WITH NAILS, GEARS. WHAT CAUSES THAT, SIR?
CANISTER SHOT, MA'AM.
WHEN AMMUNITION IS LOW, A SHELL IS LOADED WITH SCRAP METAL OF ALL DESCRIPTION AND FIRED ONTO TROOPS FROM A CANNON.

BUT THAT'S HORRIBLE! OUR YOUNG BOYS CUT DOWN BY SECESSIONIST... TRASH!
AND THEIR BOYS BY OURS, MA'AM.
NO! I CAN'T BELIEVE THAT! THE UNION IS RIGHTEOUS AND 'TIS A HOLY MISSION THEY'RE ABOUT.

IT'S NICE TO THINK THAT. I USED TO THINK IT, BUT I'VE SEEN THE ELEPHANT NOW, AND THE WAY OF IT IS...
MA'AM, WE'RE JUST TRYING TO KILL ALL OF THEM BEFORE THEY KILL ALL OF US.
PRIVATE MORRIS! THE BANDAGES?

I AM SORRY, NURSE FRANCES, IF MY MAN HAS BEEN TROUBLING YOU.
NO TROUBLE, CORPORAL. NO TROUBLE AT ALL.

GOOD DAY, MA'AM.

THAT ACCENT--SHE'S NOT AMERICAN, IS SHE?
NEVER MIND THAT, SON. FIRST YOU'RE GOIN' TEACH ME YOUR MYSTIC WAYS.

WHAT CAN YOU MEAN?
NIGH ON TWO WEEKS I'M RUNNING WOUNDED AND SUPPLIES TWIXT THAT HOSPITAL AND CAMP, AND THAT LITTLE LASS AIN'T SPOKE BUT TEN WORDS TO ME.
MOST OF 'EM TODAY!
BUT A MOMENT IN YOUR MAGIC PRESENCE AND SHE'S CHATTIN', MAKIN' COW EYES. WHILE YOU TALKIN' 'BOUT KILLIN'!
SPEAK TRUE, VIRGIL. WHAT DEVIL GAVE YOU THIS POWER?

YOU'VE BEEN TOO LONG IN THE SUN, LEVON. THAT'S MY THINKING.
MY THINKIN' IS YOU OUGHT BE HAPPY FOR THE TIME YOU SPENT WITH LOVELY NURSE SHAW.

'CAUSE I TELL YOU PLAIN, IT'S LIKE TO BE A COON'S AGE 'FORE I LET YOU ANYWHERES NEAR HER AGAIN.

CRACK CRACK CRACK!
WHAT IN HELL?!

"GUNFIRE!"
THE FILTHY SECESH IS A'COMIN'! MOVE OUT, BOYS! MOVE OUT!

HOLD STEADY, HOLD STEADY! JUST A SKIRMISH. NO TIME TO LOSE YOUR NERVE.

THESE REBS MERELY TRY TO DRAW US OUT. STAND YOUR GROUND AND DROP 'EM IN THEIR TRACKS!

NOT IF I DROP YOU INTO HELL FIRST, BLUEBELLY!

HYAAH!!

QUITE AN ENTRANCE, CORPORAL HATLO! AND TIMELY.
IS THIS THE REBEL PUSH?
NOT ENOUGH JOHNNYS FOR THAT, I'D SAY. MORE LIKELY A ROGUE COMPANY WHAT IS ON ITS OWN HOOK.

DRIVE 'EM BACK, BOYS!
A FEW DOZEN HOTHEADS WHO CAN'T WAIT TO DIE! LET'S OBLIGE 'EM!

WE GOT 'EM NOW, BROTHERS! AIN'T BUT HALF OUT OF THEIR SUPPER DISHES!!
THESE BLACK REPUBLICANS WILL LAY IT DOWN SOON, OH YES!
CRACK!

ACE SHOOTIN', CHIEF! THROUGH THE BREADBASKET AND THAT DOG'S *DONE!*
THEY GOT THE CAP'N, MEN! LIGHT OUT! LIGHT OUT!!
THEY'S ON THE RUN NOW!! WICKED COWARDS SURELY GON' DIE TODAY!!

"CUT 'EM ALL DOWN!"

CRAK!

HEAR ME, REBS!

CRACK!
YOU AIN'T FIT FO' BATTLE!
NO MORALS, NO SENSE, NO COURAGE!
WHIIIIZ!

LIKE THIS LITTLE GRAY CALF HERE, CAUGHT IN THE "SAVAGE TEETH"... OF A PASTURE FENCE!
KEEP FLAPPIN' THEM GUMS, APE. I'LL GIT ME A BEAD ON YOU YIT!
SERGEANT McBRIDE, THE MAJOR'S LOOKING FOR YOU. BEST WE GET OUT OF RANGE OF THE ENEMY, YES?
WHAT'S 'AT? OH, PRIVATE MORRIS! BUT THERE AIN'T PURPOSE TO WORRY!
THEM GRAYBACKS AIN'T LIKE YOU. CAIN'T HIT THE EARTH WITH A SHOTGUN.
FACT, WHY'N'T YOU PICK THEM JOHNNYS OFF YO'SE'F?
WHHHIIZ
MISTUH, HE'S BOUND TO GET US ALL KILT! CAN YOU TALK TO HIM?
WHAT DO YOU SAY, SERGEANT? SHALL WE GET THE PRISONER BACK TO CAMP, SEE WHAT HE KNOWS?
WE FIGHTIN' A WAR, PRIVATE.

BLAM
BLAM
BLAM
NO PRISONERS!

IT WAS A MERCY KILLING, REBS! THAT LITTLE VEAL WON'T PISS HISSELF SCARED NO MO'!

CRAK!

RECKON THAT'LL SHUT HIS SINNIN' MOUTH.

HHHHHH...
SERGEANT? ARE YOU HIT BAD?
BAD, PRIVATE?
NO.
NOT BAD.

CHRIST GOD! I SWEAR I DRILLED HIS HEART!

THEM BOYS SHOT YO' SERGEANT, *CHIEF!* PEEL THAT EAGLE EYE O' YOURN AND RETURN FIRE.
NO. NO. I'M IN ANOTHER NIGHTMARE.

OBEY, MAN! OBEY AND KILL!
A NIGHTMARE-- OR THE FIGHTING HAS FINALLY BROKEN ME!
NO, TWO MOONS. THIS IS THE BEAST AS HE *IS*, YOU SEE TRUTH.

AT LAST-- AND WHILE YOU LIVE--YOU SEE TRUTH.

BACK!
SSSSATAN!!

YOUR LIMBS KNOW BETTER THAN YOUR HEAD, NATIVE SON.
WHAT?! WHAT DO THEY KNOW?!!
THEY KNOW MY PATH TO THE SOUTHERN SKIES!

AS I KNOW MINE ON EARTH!
HE RUNS THE ROAD OF SLAUGHTER, GRANDSON.

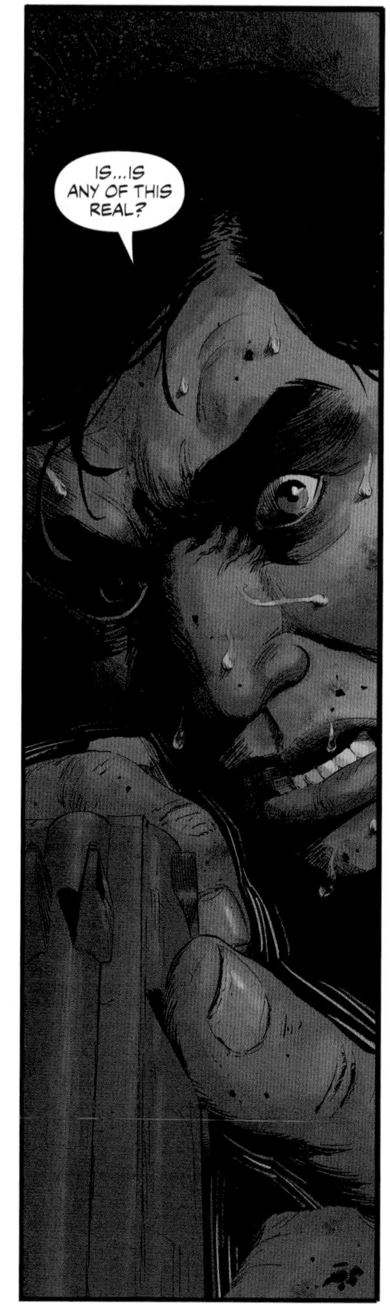
IS...IS ANY OF THIS REAL?

CRAK!

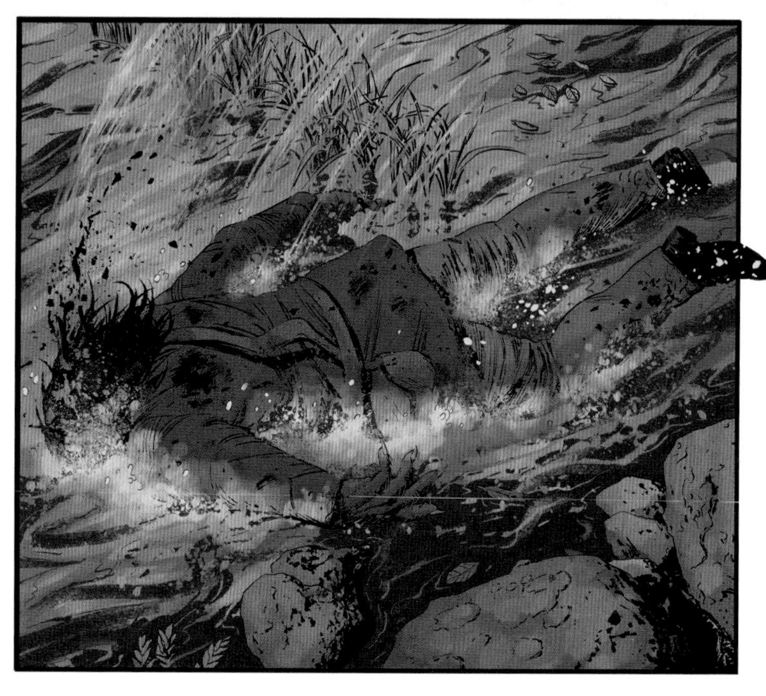

LORD GOD FORGIVE ME.
NO, PRIVATE.
MURDERING TRAITORS AREN'T ALLOWED SUCH GRACE, I DON'T BELIEVE.
BUT YOU'LL KNOW SOON ENOUGH!

PART 2

DON'T SLOW DOWN, CHIEF, OR THIS BAYONET MIGHT COULD SLIP IN BETWEEN YER RIBS.
I'M TELLING YOU, LOOK AT McBRIDE'S BODY!
WE'D BE BURYING SERGEANT McBRIDE RIGHT NOW IF HE HADN'T WASHED DOWNRIVER.
SO QUIT THE FAIRY STORIES, VIRGIL.
WON'T MAKE IT NONE EASIER FOR ANY OF US. NOW SIT YOURSELF DOWN THERE.
WHY WE EVEN DOIN' THIS? WE SEEN WHAT HE DID! GOT THE ROPE RIGHT CH'ERE, SO IT'S A HANGIN' PARTY WE SHOULD BE HAVIN'!
YOU'RE IN THE UNITED STATES ARMY, PRIVATE! THAT'S WHY!
AND IF THAT'S NOT A GOOD ENOUGH REASON FOR YOU, WE'LL LASH YOU TO THAT TREE, TOO!
YES SIR, MAJOR.

LEVON, COME ON! YOU KNOW ME.
DO I, VIRGIL?
ONE THING I DO KNOW IS, BEST TO KEEP THIS WELL OUT OF YOUR REACH.
GOOD WORK, CORPORAL. YOU TAKE THE WAGON AND RIDE OUR WOUNDED IN TO STERRETT, NOW.
YES SIR.
BUT BE BACK BY NIGHTFALL.
THERE'LL BE A COURT MARTIAL IN THE MORNING.

NURSE FRANCES, *MORPHINE!*
ON THE WAY, DOCTOR--

CORPORAL? YOU AGAIN?
YES'M. SKIRMISH AS WE RODE BACK TO CAMP. EIGHT DEAD, SIX WOUNDED.

AND-- AND PRIVATE MORRIS?

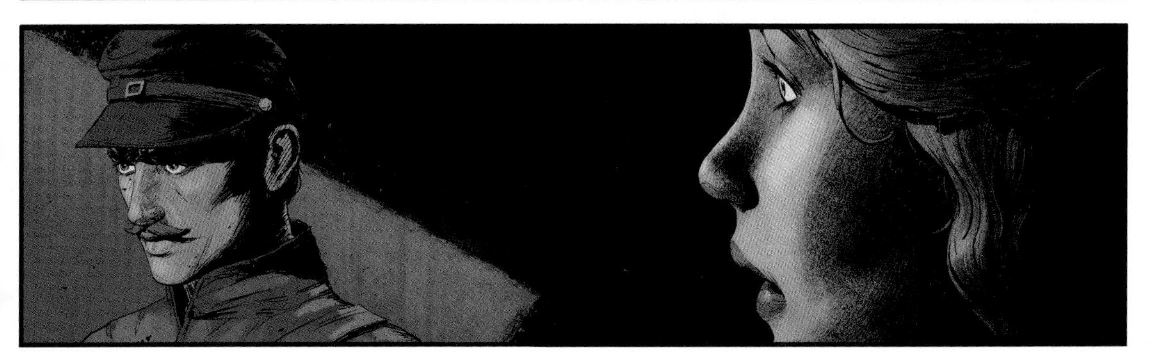

I DON'T SEE...
HOW IS THERE ANY SENSE IN IT? PRIVATE MORRIS, HE SEEMED SO CALM. LEVELHEADED, HE WAS.
PEOPLE GO LOCO IN WAR. I HEARD ABOUT IT PLENTY.
OR MAYBE THIS WAS NEVER VIRGIL'S FIGHT.
HE WAS BORN A PAWNEE, AFTER ALL. SEE, HIS FOLKS DIED FROM THE SMALLPOX.
ELGIN MORRIS AND HIS WIFE TOOK HIM IN, ELGIN BEING THE SCHOOLMASTER.
THAT'S WHERE WE MET, NIGH ON TWELVE YEARS BACK. KNOWN HIM EVER SINCE. OR... WELL, I QUESTION EVER KNOWING HIM.

ARE YE' SUGGESTIN' SIMPLY BECAUSE HE'S INDIAN, IT MAKES HIM A COLD-BLOODED KILLER?
I DON'T HAVE TO SUGGEST ANYTHING! I *SAW* HIM PUT A BULLET IN THE BACK OF A MAN'S HEAD. A MAN RUNNING AWAY!

BUT...YOU ARE RIGHT. SENSE IT DOES NOT MAKE.
A PUZZLE, AND A SAD ONE. BUT I'M TOO WEARY--AND TOO ANGRY--TO TRY TO UNLOCK IT NOW. IT'S HOME FOR ME, CORPORAL.

AND I'M THINKIN' YE' BEST RIDE OUT, TOO--IF YE' WANT TO STAY AHEAD O' THAT STORM.

NEXT TIME YOU GOT A THOUGHT ABOUT HANGIN', YOU JUS' KEEP THAT TO YER DAMN SE'F!

WHAT, YOU BELIEVE OTHER TENTS IS DRYER'N THIS 'UN? OR D'YA THINK THE MAJOR BROUGHT THE RAIN JUST TO PUNISH *YOU?*
NO, BUT HE *DID* PUT US ON WATCH. AND IF HE DON'T DO THAT, YEH, I'D BE WET--

--BUT LEAST I'D BE SLEEPING.

TWO MOONS.

DO YOU KNOW ME?
COYOTE.
AND DO YOU KNOW YOURSELF, TWO MOONS? SON OF SEES SO FAR AND SHINING WATER, GRANDSON OF HE WHO WEEPS FOR HEAVEN.
THIS IS... IT'S A DREAM. NONE OF THIS CAN BE REAL.
LIKE LEVON SAYS, FAIRY STORIES.

YOU DENY YOURSELF, TWO MOONS.
BECAUSE I HAVEN'T BEEN *"TWO MOONS"* SINCE I WAS A BOY, AND TOMORROW I'LL DIE VIRGIL MORRIS.
TONIGHT YOU WILL SEE A WAY TO LIFE. THE WHITE MAN HAS MADE CREATION SMALL TO YOUR EYES, BLINDED YOU. BUT, IN THE MORNING YOU WILL SEE MORE.
IN TWO MORNINGS--
--YOU SEE ***ALL.***

LOOK FOR THE MAN IN THE SKY.
WHAT? WHAT ARE-- A CONSTELLATION?

THE MAN IN THE SKY.
ASK THE MAN IN THE SKY.

ASK THE MAN IN THE SKY.
THE MAN IN THE SKY. THE MAN IN THE SKY.
SEE THE WAY TO LIFE.
SHUT UP! SHUT UP!

CRAA-AAK!!

HYAH, SOLDIER!
TIME T'GO!

BEST HOP ON NOW.

OR IS IT YOU GOT 'NOTHER WAY TO STAY ALIVE? *HA HA!*

SON, I 'SPECT SOME SHOOTIN' WE DON'T GIT MOVIN' RIGHT QUICK.

"SO WHAT'S IT GON' BE?"

RAIN BE LETTIN' UP. EASIER TO SEE OUR WAY NOW--BUT FOR THE YANKS, TOO.
I DIDN'T SAY, BUT THANK YOU. BUT... BUT WHY?

OH, NOW WE HEERD ON YOU. TWO OF OUR GOOD JOHNNIES SAW YOU SHOOT DOWN A UNION SERGEANT BY THE KATIT RIVER.
SAW YOU GIT TIED UP, TOO--AND COME TOL' CAP'N THESHAM ALL 'BOUT IT. SOON'S HE HEERD THAT, HE WEREN'T 'BOUT TO LET YOU GET YO' NECK STRETCHED, NO SUH!

THEN YOU'RE WITH THESHAM'S IRREGULAR COMPANY.
"IRREG'LAR." S'A WAR, AIN'T IT? S'ALL TH' WHOLE THING "IRREG'LAR."

AW, NOW I KNOW WE ON THE CORRECT TRAIL.
PASSED BY THIS LONESOME ONE ON THE WAY IN.

BY THE WAY, SERGEANT HAYES AT YO' SERVICE, AND THIS BIG FELLER IS FIRST LIEUTENANT KARCH.
AND LIKE I'S SAYIN', OUR CAP'N TOL' US WE HAD...
SAY, NOW. WHERE YOU GOIN'?
SHIT, WE ALREADY CHECKED. T'AIN'T A PENNY ON 'IM.
HUSH, KARCH. I DON'T GUESS OUR BOY'S LOOKIN' FO' MONEY.

YOU ARE ON THE CORRECT PATH, TWO MOONS.

YOU SEE A LITTLE MORE NOW. UNDERSTAND A LITTLE MORE. BUT THERE IS NOTHING YOU CAN FIND IN MY EYES.

LOOK AT THE EARTH BELOW ME.

DO YOU SEE, TWO MOONS? *DO* YOU UNDERSTAND?

WHEN YOU COME TO THE ROAD WHERE THE DEAD TRAVEL FASTER THAN THE LIVING, SIT.
SIT, AND EAT, AND ALL THAT IS IN THE SHADOWS, WHAT YOU KNOW IS THERE, WILL BE SEEN.
NO.
NO. I DON'T WANT THAT AT ALL.

I DON'T WANT TO SEE ANY OF IT!
LEAVE ME ALONE!
MISFORTUNES DO NOT FLOURISH ON ONLY THE PATH YOU SEE. THEY GROW EVERYWHERE.
YOU **SHALL** SEE, BECAUSE YOU MUST SEE.
AND WHEN YOU SEE--WHEN **YOU** SEE--
--ACT!

OH, LOOK. THOUGHT MEBBE YOU'D DIED ON ME, SON.
BREAKFAST IN A BIT, COFFEE NOW.
THANKS. HOW DID I GET HERE?
DON'T REMEMBER? MAKES SENSE, I GUESS. YOU WUZ DELIRIOUS, TALKIN' LOCO. PASSED OUT SOON'S WE GOT TO CAMP.
THE OTHERS?
OFF T'GET SUPPLIES. WEREN'T QUIET 'BOUT IT NEITHER, BUT YOU KEP' SAWIN' WOOD.

THAT'S FOX RIDGE. STILL IN THE EAST.
DIDN'T RIDE FAR FROM THE UNION CAMP AT ALL.

AHH, JUS' LIKE I FIGGERED. YOU PAWNEE!
YANKS COMIN' DOWN HERE--HELL, MOST REBS, TOO--THEY CAN'T FIND THEY ASSES WITH BOTH HANDS, A MAP, AND A COMPASS!
YEH, WE CIRCLED BACK T'THROW THE BLUE COATS OFF. WORKED, TOO.

THAT WOULD PUT US WITHIN THREE MILES OF STERRETT.
TO THE NORTH.
LIKE I SAID, SUPPLIES.

LISTEN, I WASN'T RAISED PAWNEE.
STUDIED SURVEYING SINCE I WAS A BOY, THAT'S ALL.
OKAY, MEBBE YOU AIN'T PAWNEE, BUT YOU IS GOT A NAME, RIGHT?

YES. IT'S VIRGIL--
POP
POP
BANG
POP

GUNFIRE. COMING FROM STERRETT.
WHERE YOUR SQUAD IS GETTING SUPPLIES?
UHHHH...

WAIT, NOW. HOLD ON! WHAT THE HELL--?
LORD JESUS CHRIST, SON. YOU CAN'T JUST--GODDAMMIT, BOY--
"--THAT'S MAH HORSE!"

BLAM
BLAM
BLAM
N-NO NEED FOR THAT, SIR. WE'RE MOVING FAST AS WE'RE ABLE.
MAH LIEUTENANT DISAGREES. HAH HAAAAA!
HAH HAAA. THA'S RIGHT, JAYHAWK! RUN!

CALEB, THESE ARE THE LAST OF THE EXCAVATING TOOLS.

WHERE DO YOU WANT THEM?

NAW, NAW, SWEE'PEA. GIRLS AIN' S'POSED TO WORK. SET THA' MESS DOWN AND LE'S GO FOR A WALK.

BOOM!

IF YOU'RE NOT LETTING GO O' HER IN TEN SECONDS, THE OTHER BARREL WILL BE ALL YOURS!

ONE BARREL'S **ALL** YOU GOT.

AND THEY'S SEVEN OF US.

THINK YOU **HAD** TROUBLE? PULL THA' TRIGGUH, YOU HAVE A **LOT** MORE.

NOT FROM YOU.

GODDAMN YOU, LIEUTENANT! YOU WERE TO KEEP AN EYE ON THE HORSES!
NOW THEY'VE BEEN CUT LOOSE AN' SPOOKED!

STOP YOUR GAMES AND ROUND 'EM UP.
NURSE FRANCES.
EASY! EASY. IT'S ME, VIRGIL. REMEMBER?
I CUT THE HORSES LOOSE AS A DISTRACTION.

DID YE NOW? WELL, IF IT'S A "*THANK YOU*" YER AFTER, GET THAT OUT O' YOUR HEAD.
I NEVER ASKED FOR ANY O' YOUR HELP, AND I CERTAINLY DON'T NEED IT.
I CAN SEE THAT.

BUT I NEED YOURS.

PART 3

NURSE FRANCES, A LOT OF CRAZY THINGS HAVE HAPPENED THAT I CAN'T REALLY EXPLAIN--NOT THAT YOU'D BELIEVE ME ANYWAY.
BUT I NEED YOUR HELP.
WOULDN'T I BELIEVE YOU? OR DO Y'THINK I DON'T KNOW WHAT YE'VE BEEN UP TO?
THOUGH HOW IT IS YOU COME TO BE RIDING FREE IS A MYSTERY. I HEARD YOU WERE IN ROPES.

OKAY, SO YOU KNOW I WAS ARRESTED, BUT I'M DESPERATE.
THEY WERE GOING TO HANG ME. I *HAD* TO ESCAPE.

AYE, INDEED THEY WERE. AND FOR WHAT YE'VE DONE, THAT SEEMS RIGHT ENOUGH.
DIDN'T CORPORAL HATLO TELL ME YOU WERE A COLD-BLOODED KILLER?

MA'AM, IF YOU CAN LOOK AT ME AND SEE A KILLER, THEN I GUESS I'M WASTING MY TIME.

STILL HAVEN'T WRANGLED YOUR ANIMALS?
EASY 'NUFF TRACKIN' 'EM IN THIS SLOP, BUT THEY'S BEIN' UNSOCIAL.
IS THIS A JOKE TO YOU, LIEUTENANT KARCH?
HOW FUNNY WILL IT BE WHEN YOU GO BACK TO STERRETT AND GRAB A FEW OF THEIR HORSES AS REPLACEMENTS?

BACK TO STERRETT? BUT NOW THEY'LL BE READY FOR US.
NOT US. YOU! AND I DON'T IMAGINE IT WILL BE A WARM WELCOME.

SOMETHING YOU LIKELY SHOULD'VE THOUGHT ON BEFORE YOU LEFT OUR BEASTS UNATTENDED TO SHOOT UP THE TOWN, YES?

!
HOLD ON THERE FOR A MOMENT, CAPTAIN.
"NOBODY HAS TO GO BACKWARDS."
DIDN'T REALIZE WE'D SPRUNG SUCH A GOOD HORSEMAN. BUT WHAT BROUGHT YOU AWAY FROM CAMP, MISTER...?
MORRIS. VIRGIL MORRIS. I HEARD GUNFIRE COMING FROM STERRETT. I REASONED YOU MIGHT BE IN TROUBLE, AND SINCE YOU SAVED ME FROM THE NOOSE...
A MAN OF HONOR. AND YOU RODE TO OUR AID UNARMED.
WHAT DO YOU THINK IS WORTH MORE, LIEUTENANT? A CAREFUL MAN WITH NO GUN OR A RECKLESS MAN WITH TWO?

WHAT'S THIS THEN? NO WAGON, NO SUPPLIES?
HAD TO LEAVE IT ALL BEHIND. STANDS TO REASON IF MORRIS HEARD KARCH'S GUNSHOTS, THE UNION CAMP NORTH OF STERRETT MIGHT HAVE AS WELL. WE'RE JUST LUCKY TO HAVE ALL OUR HORSES.

MUCH OBLIGED FOR LENDING MORRIS YOUR MOUNT, SERGEANT HAYES.
DIDN'T 'ZACTLY LEAVE ME NO SELECTION IN THE MATTER, DID YOU, PRIVATE?

FACT IS, YOU BEIN' IN SECH A HURRY, YOU DROPPED THIS FROM YER JACKET.
I'D FORGOTTEN ALL ABOUT THIS.

DON'T GO SO FAR IN THE WAY O' VITTLES, BUT I'LL ALLOW AS IT HAS OTHER PROPERTIES, DON'T IT?

JUS' LIKE A PRAIRIE NIGRAH. SIT ROUN', GET HOPPED UP.

SHOULDN'T YOU BE THANKING THAT MAN, LIEUTENANT? RATHER THAN INSULTING HIS HERITAGE?
OR IS IT YOU WANT TO WALK YOUR WAY BACK TO MISSOURI?
NOW PREPARE FOR THE TRIP.
GODDAMN REDSKIN...

AND I HAVE TO SAY, WITHOUT SUPPLIES, WE NEED TO GET RIGHT ON THAT.
FOR MY PART, I FEEL OUR ACCOUNTS ARE BALANCED. YOU ARE FREE TO GO, BUT IF YOU CARE TO RIDE ON TO MISSOURI WITH US, I WOULD CHEER THAT DECISION.
IT'S CLEAR THAT I'M UNWELCOME HERE IN KANSAS, CAPTAIN THESHAM.
EVERYTHING TELLS ME I'M ON THE RIGHT PATH.

"THEN WE RIDE HARD FOR THE NISHOKE RIVER. THAT WILL GET US JUST A FEW MILES FROM THE BORDER.
"WE RIDE LIKE THE DEVIL IS ON OUR TRAIL.
"AND I'M NOT ONE TO SAY THAT HE WON'T BE.
"WE RIDE HARD, WE CROSS THAT RIVER BY EVENING, AND WE'LL BE JUST FINE."

LAST NIGHT'S STORM MUST HAVE BEEN WORSE UP NORTH. NO WAY TO MAKE IT ACROSS THAT.
WE'LL BIVOUAC FOR THE NIGHT.

A ROAD WHERE THE DEAD TRAVEL FASTER THAN THE LIVING...

WHA'S 'AT, VIRG?
I SAID, I'D LIKE TO STAY HERE BY THE RIVER FOR A BIT, IF NONE OF YOU MINDS.
NOBODY GIVE A SHIT WHUT YOU DO, BOY.

WHAT DID THAT SPIRIT SAY?
"WHEN YOU COME TO WHERE THE DEAD TRAVEL FASTER THAN THE LIVING, SIT AND EAT, AND ALL WILL BE SEEN."

MAYBE... MAYBE I'M NOT LOSING MY MIND.
TIME TO FIND OUT.

NOWA, PITKU PAHS.

I DON'T KNOW WHAT I BELIEVE.
NOW YOU BELIEVE, DON'T YOU? YOU ATE THE GOD-FLOWER BECAUSE YOU BELIEVE.
BELIEVE YOUR EYES, TWO MOONS. THEY ARE OPEN NOW.

YOU SEE MORE THAN YOU DID, MORE THAN OTHERS CAN SEE, BECAUSE THERE IS MORE TO BE SEEN.
IN THIS TIME, THE SPIRIT WORLD IS STRONG. THE NAHURAC ARE NEAR--BUT THE SEHSEKACHAN, THE EVIL ONES, THE ANGRY ONES, CANNOT BE CONTROLLED.
WAR BRINGS THEM TO LIFE, INTO THIS WORLD. THE EVIL WILL ALWAYS BE STRONGEST THEN.
BUT THIS WAR OF THE WHITE MEN GOES ON FOR YEARS. THOUSANDS DIE, BROTHERS KILL BROTHERS AND THE DYING SOULS, FAT WITH THE VENOM OF HATRED, FEED THE GREEDY SEHSEKACHAN.
SUCKING PAIN AND RESENTMENT FROM THOSE DAMNED SPIRITS, GROWING STRONGER.
THEY MASK IN HUMAN SKIN, BUT YOU WILL SEE THEM NOW. FROM YOU THEY CANNOT HIDE.

LEAD CANNOT KILL THEM. FIRE CANNOT KILL THEM.
IRON, TWO MOONS! YOU WERE TOLD BEFORE, BUT YOU CAN HEAR ME NOW. ONLY AN IRON BLADE WILL END THEIR LIVES.

THEY ARE NEAR, TWO MOONS. THEY ARE WITH YOU NOW!

ATIUS TIRAWA WATCHES OVER YOU.

HEY, VIRG. GOT WORRIED 'BOUT YOU. BRUNG YOU A LITTLE CHOW. AN' A LITTLE DEE-FENSE, TOO.
'CUZ KARCH AIN'T THE ONLY COYOTE ROUND THESE PARTS.

THOUGH HE BE THE MEANEST.
DANG IT, VIRG. WHUT YOU GONE AND DONE THAT FER?!

MY KNIFE...
"KNIFE"?

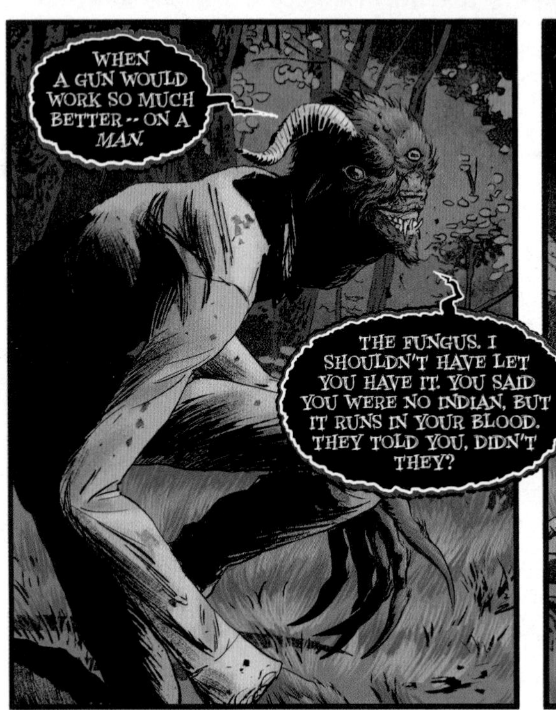
WHEN A GUN WOULD WORK SO MUCH BETTER -- ON A *MAN*.
THE FUNGUS. I SHOULDN'T HAVE LET YOU HAVE IT. YOU SAID YOU WERE NO INDIAN, BUT IT RUNS IN YOUR BLOOD. THEY TOLD YOU, DIDN'T THEY?

YOU SEE ME NOW, MEDICINE MAN. YOU KNOW A GUN'S NO GOOD ON ME.

BUT IT CAN KILL YOU DEAD!

THWUNK!
WHAT THE HELL?
DOWN BY THE RIVER!
DID THE "GREAT SPIRIT" TELL YOU A STICK COULD HURT ME, MEDICINE MAN?
NO.

BUT IT WILL KEEP YOU BUSY UNTIL THE OTHERS GET HERE.

EVEN A PACK OF BRUTES LIKE THEM WILL HELP ME WHEN THEY SEE YOU AS YOU ARE.

HA HA HA HA HA HA HA HA HA HA

SORRY, HAYES. COULDN'T RISK SHOOTIN'. MIGHTA HIT YA.
COFF-- JUS'--CHOKE-- JUS' LONG AS YOU GOT HERE IN TIME...
JUST IN TIME TO FINISH OFF THAT INJUN RAT--
WHUT...?
KARCH, WHERE'S YOUR OTHER IRON?

BANG
BANG
BANG
BANG
BANG
BANG

HEE HEH HEEEEE!
JESUS, GABBY! QUIT THAT! HE MEANS TO KILL US ALL!

AHA HAHAHA HAHA!

THAT INDIAN BOY'S GONE LOCO! WE STICK AROUND, HE'S LIKE TO TAKE THE LOT OF US!
OR MAYBE HE JUST WANTS GABBY.

I SAY, LET HIM HAVE HIM!

WAIT NOW, CAP'N THESHAM! YOU CAIN'T LEAVE WITHOUT YOU GOT YER COOK!

GAH!

IS IT YOUR PLAN TO SHOOT ME, MEDICINE MAN?

THIS HOG LEG HERE IS MADE OF IRON, ISN'T IT? MAKES A GOOD BLUDGEON. COULD BE I NEED AN IRON *BLADE* TO KILL YOU.

BUT LET'S JUST SEE.

DROP THAT WEAPON, PRIVATE MORRIS.
YOU ARE MY PRISONER.

PART 4

THAT'S IT, MEN. KEEP THE PRESSURE UP.

THESE REBS WILL DIE, OR RUN!

BY HEAVEN, I BELIEVE WE'VE GOT 'EM!

McCAY, WHY DO YOU STOP?
I AM ADDRESSING YOU, PRIVATE! WHAT DO YOU THINK--

SMASH!
McCAY, HAS THE LIEUTENANT BEEN HIT?

BLAM
BLAM
BLAM
BLAM
BLAM
BLAM

ALL RIGHT, MEN. WE ARE DOWN FOR THE NIGHT-- AND IF TWO DAYS' RIDE FOR ONLY TWO MEN HARDLY SEEMS WORTH IT, YOU WILL RECALL WE OWED IT TO SERGEANT McBRIDE.
CORPORAL, GET THE PRISONERS INTO LOCKUP. COME MORNING YOU'LL ESCORT THE REBEL TO THE COURTHOUSE IN AHERN.
MAYBE... MAYBE MY MIND *IS* UNSOUND. NOBODY ELSE CAN SEE WHAT I SEE, AND NONE OF IT *EVER* MADE SENSE.
THEM "FOOLISH MUSHROOMS"-- S'WHUT MY PAPPY CALLED 'EM-- YOU EAT 'EM, VIRJ, AND YOUR MIND GETS LOCO.
BUT NOT FER MUCH LONGER.

QUIET! BOTH OF YOU.
AND MISS FRANCES, IT'S MY OPINION YOU SHOULD GO TO YOUR HOME. THERE WAS NO NEED FOR YOU TO HAVE ACCOMPANIED US IN THE FIRST PLACE.
NO NEED, Y'SAY? WELL, IT'S *MY* OPINION THERE WAS A GREAT NEED.

YE PAINTED VIRGIL AS A VICIOUS TRAITOR, BUT WHEN THE GUERILLAS RAVAGED THIS TOWN, HE DIDN'T COME T'HELP 'EM. NOT AT ALL.
THOSE BOYS DIDN'T GET THEIR SUPPLIES, SO I EXPECT THEY'LL RIDE STRAIGHT FOR MISSOURI.
ALL THAT SHOOTING SHALL BRING MEN FROM MY COMPANY SOON. IF YOU TELL THEM TO LOOK FOR TRACKS OF EIGHT MOUNTS RIDING EAST, THEY'RE SURE TO CATCH UP TO US, AND THESE MEN WILL HANG.
BUT THEIR HORSES YE CUT LOOSE. WHAT IF THEY DON'T CATCH 'EM ALL? THEY'RE BOUND TO RETURN FOR MORE.
THEY WON'T CATCH THEM ALL, BUT I WILL. THEY WILL NOT COME BACK, MA'AM.
JAIL
AND SO I TOLD YE ALL THAT, BUT I WASN'T ABOUT TO LET YE HUNT HIM DOWN AND SHOOT HIM LIKE THE ANIMAL YE SEEM TO THINK HE IS.
NURSE, IT WAS MY OWN EYES THAT SAW THIS MAN MURDER ONE OF MY SERGEANTS AND I DIDN'T SHOOT HIM ON SIGHT THEN.
THAT IS NOT HOW WE DO THINGS IN THIS ARMY. LOOK TO THE REBS FOR THAT KIND OF SAVAGERY.

"THE SAME REBS THAT KILLED YOUR SHERIFF.
"PRIVATE MORRIS WILL SIT IN YOUR JAIL TONIGHT, AND COME MORNING HE'LL FACE A COURT MARTIAL."
GRANDFATHER, WHAT HAVE YOU DONE TO ME?
TALKIN' TO DEAD FOLK? SON, I DONE TOL' YOU, S'THE MUSHROOM. ONCE IT WEARS OFF, YOU BE JUS' LIKE ER'BODY ELSE AGAIN.
YOU'RE LYING.
I AM.
ON THE BRINK OF MADNESS ALL YOUR DAYS-- HEARING GHOSTS, DOUBTING YOUR VISION-- BUT THINK HOW LUCKY YOU ARE.
WHAT?
YOU ARE *LEARNING*, TWO MOONS! AND SO YOUNG. HAVE YOU SEEN EVEN TWENTY-FIVE SUNS?
I CRAWLED IN THE BASEMENT OF THE ABYSS BEFORE MAN STRUNG HIS FIRST BOW.
YOUR OLDEST CHIEFS? AS MAYFLIES TO ME. THIS WORLD IS THE SMALLEST PART OF *ALL* THAT IS.
AND NOW, THE FABRIC HAS BEEN TORN. YOU PEER IN, TWO MOONS. WHAT DO YOU SEE?

"MORE THAN MOST PEOPLE CAN EVER HOPE FOR IS YOURS, AND STILL...MERE GLIMPSES!
"A BEAST THAT BREATHES A FEW DECADES, HOW CAN IT HOPE TO RECOGNIZE ALL THE MIRACLES OF THE UNIVERSE?
"WITH BUT A LUMP OF FLESH IN IT'S SKULL, HOW COULD IT EVER COME TO UNDERSTAND THEM?"

IT'S A GIFT FOR YOU, TWO MOONS.
A GIFT FOR THE SHAMAN, FOR THE HOLY MAN-- THE *SEER!*
BLAZES, REB! YOU WERE DIPPING IN SOME POWERFUL WHISKY BEFORE WE GOT TO YOU, IS MY GUESS.
NURSE FRANCES IS A KIND SOUL AND WANTS TO TEND YOUR WOUND, VIRGIL.
THE MAJOR RELENTED TO HER PETITION, PERHAPS TO PROVE HIS CIVILITY. DON'T YOU MAKE US OUT FOOLS, BOY, OR I SWEAR--

YER CORPORAL'S A PRAT. AS IF YE COULD HURT ME THROUGH THOSE BARS-- AND WITH THAT WOUND AND HANDS TIED.
...AS IF YE **WOULD** HURT ME.

THE -- THE REBEL. I HEARD HIM CALL YE "TWO MOONS"?
AND YOU HEARD LEVON. THE REBEL'S INTOXICATED.
SO THAT'S **NOT** YER NAME?
IT **WAS.** IT IS, MAYBE. I'M NOT SURE.
I CAN'T REMEMBER WHAT IT MEANS.
I'VE BEEN "VIRGIL" SINCE THE MORRIS FAMILY TOOK ME IN. I DOUBT EVEN **THEY** WOULD HAVE ME NOW.
THAT MAN -- THE OLD ONE IN THE HOSPITAL THAT DAY WE MET. YE SAID YOU DIDN'T KNOW HIM.
BUT I LIED.
HE WAS MY GRANDFATHER -- "HE WHO WEEPS FOR HEAVEN." **HIS** NAME MEANS SOMETHING.
AFTER MY PARENTS DIED, HE TRIED TO KEEP ME CONNECTED TO THE PAWNEE -- TO THEIR CULTURE. I REJECTED HIM -- HE PERSISTED.

ME DA, HE DIED WHEN I WAS YOUNG, TOO. IT SCARED ME, AND IT SCARED ME MUM.
SO, TO AMERICA WE CAME. TO ESCAPE THE FAMINE, SHE SAID, AND SURE IT WAS THAT-- BUT IT WAS A RESCUE SHE WAS AFTER. FROM FEAR, AND FROM HEARTBREAK.
"T'ING IS, YE CAN'T OUTRUN SORROW, CAN YE?
"YE CAN'T GET AWAY FROM WHO YE ARE."
AIBREANN SHAW
Loving Mother
1822 –

AND I KNOW SOMETIMES THAT'S HARD.

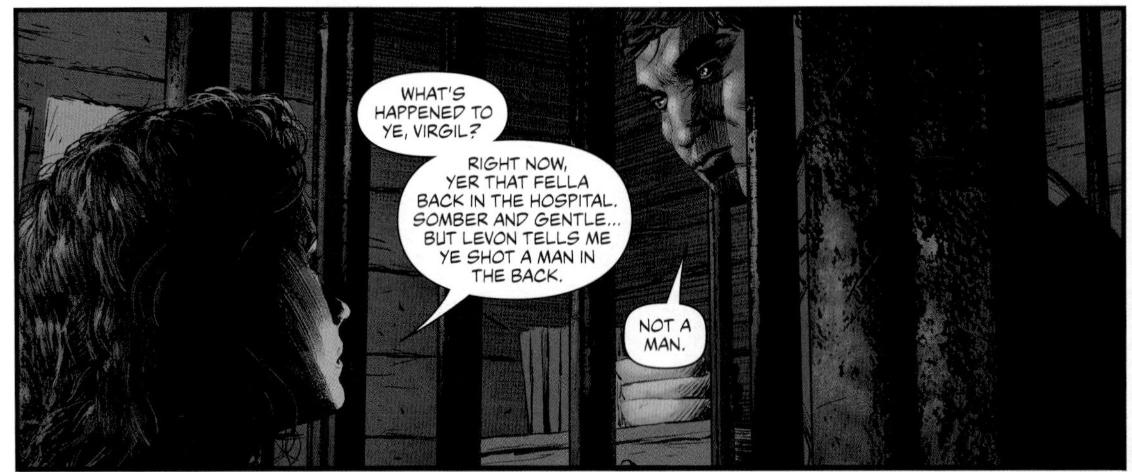
WHAT'S HAPPENED TO YE, VIRGIL?
RIGHT NOW, YER THAT FELLA BACK IN THE HOSPITAL. SOMBER AND GENTLE... BUT LEVON TELLS ME YE SHOT A MAN IN THE BACK.
NOT A MAN.

"OR I DIDN'T SEE A MAN.
"WHAT'S HAPPENED TO ME IS I'VE SEEN THINGS. DREADFUL CREATURES THAT FEED ON ANGER, ON FEAR, AND HATE. WHAT I'VE SEEN IS THAT THEY HIDE INSIDE MEN ALL AROUND US."

THESE DEMONS, OR DEVILS--WHICH, I DON'T KNOW--BUT THEY'VE COME TO STOKE HATE AND VIOLENCE IN US, FOR NO OTHER REASON THAN TO FEAST ON IT.
PARASITES OF FEAR, AND WHILE THEY FEED, THEY DRAIN COMPASSION FROM US LIKE SLIT HOGS.
VIRGIL...
DON'T YE KNOW THAT'S MAD?

IS THERE A CORPORAL LEVON HERE?
THAT WOULD BE--
OH, SORRY, LIEUTENANT. WHAT CAN I DO FOR YOU, SIR?
NOT SO MUCH, I THINK.
A GOOD DAY TO YOU, MA'AM.
LIEUTENANT McCAY, CORPORAL, OF THE SECOND DIVISION. YOUR COMMANDER DID SEND WORD TO GENERAL CARR THAT A REBEL PRISONER HERE NEEDED TRANSPORT TO AHERN. I'VE COME TO ACCOUNT THAT.
OH...BUT, MAJOR SWINNERTON GAVE ME OTHER ORDERS. I BELIEVE IT'S BEST I CHECK IN WITH HIM.
I IMAGINE HE'S SLEEPING. LET'S NOT BOTHER THE MAN.

YOU ARE NOT ACQUAINTED WITH THE MAJOR. IT'S STRICTLY BY THE BOOK IN THIS COMPANY. I SHOULDN'T SNEEZE WITHOUT ASKING PERMISSION.
HAH. WELL THEN, BY ALL MEANS, GO FIND THE MAJOR.
I'LL WAIT HERE WITH THE PRISONERS.
OH, LORD!
CLATTER
NO SCREAMING, WOMAN.
A GUNSHOT WILL BRING SOLDIERS, BUT I WILL SHOOT IF YOU DO NOT QUIETLY GRAB THAT KEY RING AND OPEN THE CELL DOOR.
OH YES, OH YES! IT'S BUST-OUT TIME!

--URK!
AH, YOU DON'T LIKE THIS, DO YOU? EVEN THIS LITTLE BLADE COULD HURT YOU.
BUT I DON'T WANT TO HURT YOU.
EEEEEEEEE!

OH, GOD! LORD JESUS! WHAT IS IT?! WHAT IS IT?!!
...HELL... IS THAT THIN'...?
YOU SEE IT, THEN? YOU BOTH SEE WHAT IT IS?

LIEUTENTANT McCAY? IS THERE A PROBLEM?
DO YOU REQUIRE ASSISTANCE?
WHAT'S GOING ON?
IS THAT MORE O' THOSE CREATURES? IS IT?
I TOLD YOU, THEY'RE ALL AROUND US. HE CALLED THEM. SOME WAY. A SIGNAL OF SOME KIND.
WHAT ARE YOU MEN DOING HERE? GET BACK TO YOUR POSTS.

SIR, THOSE AREN'T OUR BOYS!
EH? WHAT CAN YOU MEAN?
JAIL
BLAM!
BLAM BLAM
BLAM
BLAM
BLAM BLAM

SIR, IS IT BAD?
NOT SO BAD AS IT MIGHT HAVE BEEN. BROKE MY ARM, I THINK.
"WHERE THE DEVIL IS THAT NURSE?"
WHAT IS THIS ABOMINATION?
AND WHY DOES IT WEAR UNION BLUES?
IT WALKED IN HERE A MAN, MAJOR. AND THOSE UNION BOYS OUT THERE--WE THINK THEY'RE MORE OF THEM.

MAN OR BEAST, WE KNOW HOW TO HANDLE THEM.

HEE HEE HEEEEEEE!

HFFF
HRRRR
FFFF
HISSSSSSSSS!!

DAMN YOU MEN, STOP GAPING--

"--AND FIRE!"
BLAM
BLAM
BLAM
BLAM
JAIL

BLAM
BLAM
BLAM
SHREEEEE!!!
GET ME OUT OF HERE, FOR GOD'S SAKE! LET ME OUT!!!

JAIL
MAJOR SWINNERTON, RELEASE THE PRISONER.
OR I WILL LEAVE THIS TOWN A MUDDY HOLE OF ASH AND BLOOD.

PART 5

THE PRISONER MAY NOT APPEAR THREATENING AT THIS MOMENT, BUT I WOULD ASK HIS HONOR NOT TO BE DECEIVED.

THE WITNESSES WILL TELL YOU HOW THIS MAN RODE WITH A BAND OF BLACK FLAG GUERILLAS --

--THE SAME BAND THAT TORCHED WILMORE IN JUNE, KILLING THIRTY-TWO MEN, WOMEN, AND CHILDREN!

HE IS **NOT** A HARMLESS MAN. HE IS A SAVAGE -- HE IS A COLD-BLOODED KILLER.

BUT AGAIN, MY WORD IS MEANINGLESS. LISTEN TO WHAT THE WITNESSES HAVE TO SAY.

YOU LOOK AT ME AS IF YOU DIDN'T HEAR ME, MAJOR. RELEASE THE PRISONER AND WE'LL BE OFF.
WHICH PRISONER? THE CONFEDERATE GUERILLA, OR VIRGIL MORRIS?
WE'LL TAKE *BOTH*, IF YOU PLEASE.

LEVON, FOR GOD'S SAKE, LET ME OUT!
HEE HEE HEE HEE
HUSH NOW. I'M TRYING TO HEAR WHAT THE MAJOR IS SAYING.

MISS FRANCES, LISTEN TO ME. IT MAKES NO DIFFERENCE WHAT THEY'RE SAYING. THOSE EVIL SPIRITS -- THOSE DEVILS. THEY'LL SAY **ANYTHING.**

THEY CAN'T GET THROUGH THESE BARS. THEY CAN'T EVEN TOUCH IRON THE WAY THEY ARE NOW.
THEY NEED **YOU** TO UNLOCK THE CELLS FOR THEM TO GET AT HAYES HERE, AND WHEN YOU DO--

--THEY'LL KILL US ALL.
HEY!
FINE. RUN THEN. THERE'S A BACK DOOR.
JUST DON'T HURT HER.

WHY DO THEY STILL CHATTER?
LET THEM. LET THEM THINK THEY HAVE A CHOICE. THEY CAN'T MAKE SENSE OF US, OR SHOOT US DEAD. THEY'LL DO AS WE SAY.
WHAT WILL IT BE, MAJOR?
THAT THING OVER THERE...THAT WAS SERGEANT McBRIDE. ALL ALONG, THAT THING RODE WITH ME.
IT'S A GODDAMNED LIAR, MEN. ALONG WITH BEING A CREATURE FROM THE PIT. WE CAN'T BARGAIN WITH IT.
MAJOR! DO WE HAVE OUR AGREEMENT? WILL YOU LET THE PRISONER FREE?
THE PRISONER IS FREE.

THAT'S RIGHT, YOUR WAR LEADER'S GONE--AND THIS SWORD IS STEEL!
BAD MEDICINE FOR CHILDREN OF DARKNESS!!!

CRACK
BANG
POW
BLAM
BLAM
PFFT

YOU CHASED OFF THE WHOLE LOT WITH ONE SWORD. THEY MUST TRULY FEAR IRON, JUST AS YOU SAID.
BUT HOW DO THEY FIRE AT US WITH RIFLES? THE BARRELS, THE BREECHES--HELL, IT'S GOT IRON ALL OVER IT.
THE ONES FIRING THE RIFLES ARE STILL HUMAN IN FORM. WHEN YOU "KILL" THEIR HUMAN BODIES, WELL, IT JUST FALLS AWAY. I SAW IT HAPPEN TO McBRIDE.

HEE HEEEE HEEEE!

HAND ME THAT SWORD, VIRGIL! I'LL RUN THAT HYENA THROUGH AND THEY'LL HAVE NOTHING TO FIGHT FOR.
STAND DOWN, CORPORAL!
I'D DO IT MYSELF, BUT IT WON'T STOP THEM. THEY ARE THE THREAT RIGHT NOW, LEVON.

WE KILL HIM, THEY KEEP COMIN', WE **DON'T** KILL HIM, THEY KEEP COMIN', WE GIVE HIM BACK, THEY **KEEP COMIN'.**
AND MY RIFLE AIN'T WORTH A **DAMN** AGAINST THEM.

HERE, SON.
WHEN THEY CLOSE IN, BETTER IT BE IN THE HANDS OF AN ABLE-BODIED SOLDIER.

WE HAVE CANNON OUT OF THEIR RANGE WE COULD USE --AND OUR ROUNDSHOT IS IRON.
ROUNDSHOT CUTS A NARROW SWATH. AND ONCE WE START FIRING, OUR SWORDS WON'T SEEM SO TERRIBLE. THE REST WILL CHARGE.

YOU'RE NEEDIN' SUMTIN' THAT CAN HIT LOTS MORE O' 'EM AT ONCE.
YOU'RE NEEDIN' CANISTER SHOT.

MOST OF THESE SHOULD BE FILLED WITH IRON GRAPESHOT, BUT IT'S POSSIBLE WE'VE A FEW LOADED WITH NAILS AND SUCH.
BUT NAILS ARE MADE OF IRON, SO...
MISS, I'M AFRAID TO ASK, BUT HOW DID YOU KNOW ABOUT CANISTER? ABOUT THE DISPERSAL OF PROJECTILES?
I'M A NURSE, MAJOR SWINNERTON. NEAR THE FRONT LINES, I'VE BEEN. I KNOW MORE ABOUT CANISTER THAN I EVER WANTED TO.
AIM LOW SO THE CANISTER HITS THE GROUND IN FRONT OF THEM.
THE SPRAY OF FLACK WILL BE WIDEST THEN.
THIS I FOUND IN THE DRAWER OF THE JAILHOUSE. CORPORAL HATLO SAID IT WOULD BE YOURS?
IT'S MY HOPE YOUR QUICK THINKING MAY MAKE THIS BLADE UNNECESSARY.
STILL, THANK YOU.

YEA!
BLAST
HURRAH!
TEAR THEM DOWN!
WELL, IT'S A BAD ENDIN' FOR THE EVIL, BUT I'M NOT ONE TO WATCH.
DEVILS THEY MAY BE, BUT THE SOUND O' THEIR DYIN' IS MORE'N I CAN STAND.

GOD, NO!
AAAAII!!!!
MISS FRANCES!

HHHHHH!

HOLD YOUR FIRE!

VIRGIL, WHAT'RE YE DOIN'? WHY DON'T YE RUN BACK?
CALM YOURSELF, MISS FRANCES. WE NEED TO GET YOU OFF THE BATTLEFIELD.

HE IS JUST ONE.
ALONE.
IS HE THE LEADER?
JUST ONE.
NO, TWO MOONS.

YOU ARE A HOLY MAN. WAR IS FOR THE OTHERS. TOO MUCH BLOOD IS ON YOU ALREADY.

AND VENOM SPILLS FROM THE VEINS OF THESE BEASTS. STAY FROM THEM, OR BE TAINTED.
NOW YOU SPEAK CLEARLY TO ME? NOW YOU WISH TO ADVISE ME?

YOU FIENDS CAME HERE FOR STRIFE?

YOU WANT HATE?

YOU THROW ME INTO THE PATH OF THESE THINGS! YOU *SHOW* THEM TO ME, ASK ME TO STOP THEM.
YOU PUT IRON BLADES INTO MY HANDS, AND YOU SAY I MUST NOT FIGHT?!

AS IF I HAD A CHOICE!

YOU WANT FEAR?

I'LL GIVE YOU FEAR!

NO, VIRGIL...

GOD, NO...

YOU WAITING FOR HIM TO DO ALL THE KILLING FOR YOU?
GET IN THERE!
SON, I COULD NOT HAVE BEEN MORE WRONG ABOUT YOU. YOU HAVE MY APOLOGIES, AS LITTLE VALUE AS THEY BE.
MISS FRANCES, MAJOR--IS SHE...?

"SHE'S WELL AND CARED FOR, PRIVATE. BUT SHE WON'T WANT TO SEE YOU LIKE THIS."
DIDJA SEE HIM? HE WAS A SAVAGE, JUST AS YOU SAID.
NOT LIKE HIM. NOT THE WAY HE WAS.
I DIDN'T SAY THAT, MISS FRANCES. AND WE ALL HAVE TO FIGHT.

HE BECAME ONE OF THEM, HE DID. LIKE A... BEAST!

BUT I NEED TO PUT THE SWORD TO THAT GUERILLA.
NO, SON. HE'LL GET HIS TRIAL, AND HE'LL HANG, WE KNOW THAT, BUT HE'S A PRISONER, NOT A COMBATANT.
MAJOR, WHY DO YOU THINK THEY CAME FOR HIM?

THEY ASKED FOR YOU TOO, PRIVATE MORRIS. WHAT WOULD YOU HAVE ME MAKE OF THAT?

I'LL SIGN A FURLOUGH FOR YOU. RIDE HOME TO YOUR FOLKS. REST. YOU'VE EARNED IT.
MY "FOLKS," MAJOR? I'LL SEE WHAT I CAN DO.

BEFORE SENTENCE IS PASSED, HAS THE PRISONER ANYTHING TO SAY IN HIS DEFENSE?

DON'T KNOW ME ANY GOOD JOKES, SO I GUESS NOT.
"YER HONOR."

SOLOMON HAYES, HAVING FOUND YOU GUILTY OF MULTIPLE COUNTS OF MURDER AND DESTRUCTION OF PROPERTY, YOU ARE SENTENCED TO BE HANGED BY THE NECK UNTIL DEAD.
REETY ALL RIGHTY!

RECKON I SEE Y'ALL AT THE HANGIN'!

WHAT DO YOU THINK WILL HAPPEN TOMORROW? WILL THE HUMAN BODY FALL AWAY, LIKE YOU SAID, OR--
YOU KNOW, BEING ON FURLOUGH, I'VE GOTTEN TO KNOW THE FOLKS HERE IN TOWN. THE SHERIFF, FOR INSTANCE? HE LOST A SISTER IN THE WILMORE MASSACRE.

ACCORDING TO HIM, THERE'S A SHORTAGE OF ROPE.
HE WAS OPEN TO SUGGESTIONS. I MADE ONE.

WELL, THAT'S THAT, THEN.

"MY FURLOUGH IS UP IN A WEEK.
"MAYBE NOT LONG ENOUGH FOR ME TO FIND WHERE MY FOLKS ARE, BUT IT'S WORTH A TRY.

"WHEN I GET BACK TO CAMP, YOU TELL ME HOW THE HANGING WENT, OKAY?

"YOU LET ME KNOW IF HAYES WAS ANY TROUBLE."

ALTERNATE COVERS

#1B BY
GERARDO ZAFFINO

#1C BY
JEFFREY VEREGGE

#1 2ND PTG ART BY
VALERIO GIANGIORDANO
COLORS BY
BILL CRABTREE

#2B ART BY
FRANCESCO MOBILI &
FRANCESCO SEGALA

#3B ART BY
RICCARDO LATINA
COLORS BY
VALENTINA BIANCONI

#4B BY
GONZALO RUGGIERI

#5B BY
ROBERTO RICCI

VERE
GGE

US

SKETCH COVERS

ART BY
VALERIO GIANGIORDANO

2021

2021

SKETCHBOOK

ART BY
VALERIO GIANGIORDANO

WITH ANNOTATION BY
JOHN ARCUDI

Layouts.

Valerio does all his layouts with word balloons included (something every comics artist should strongly consider doing!). It's really effective in helping compose panels, and leading the reader's eye both with art and word balloons. Also, how about those "splashes" of color?

Cover Concepts

First covers are always important, so Valerio worked pretty hard on getting the right image, the right feel. The black and white sketch here would absolutely have made a killer cover, but we weren't sure that it was right for the FIRST cover, so we kicked a few ideas around and when he showed me this color concept, I knew we had it. Still my favorite cover of the series!

Spirits

The opening sequence to Chapter One was tricky. Valerio played with it to get the atmosphere just right. I can't say I had a very clear idea of what that strange spirit figure that wanders the Union Army camp should look like, but when I saw this image... well, it speaks for itself.

The Coyote Spirit that appears in Chapter Two and beyond could have just been a standard coyote, I suppose, but I wanted to mess a bit with the accepted iconography because what Virgil (Two Moons) was going through was nightmarish, even hellish. He's experiencing the manifesting of his shamanism much in the way that schizophrenics experience the onset of their symptoms – usually in young adulthood. The Coyote Spirit should reflect the fear that Virgil was feeling.

Character Design

Getting the characters right is always vital. Making the characters individuals, easily identifiable even in a crowd, that's not something everybody can pull off easily. Fortunately for this project, it turned out to be one of Valerio's strengths.

Virgil (Two Moons)

Valerio got this right on the very first try. The expressiveness that runs the gamut from amusement to defiance was right there in the first drawings. And the strong Indigenous features absolutely bring Virgil to life. When I saw this, I knew Valerio was the right collaborator for the project.

Frances

In many ways Frances had to be the female equivalent to Virgil. She goes through a lot in this first arc and again, her face had to articulate a lot of emotions, but she's a survivor, a fighter. She looks like that here.

Sergeant McBride

We already had some visuals to work from for this character, but Valerio—once again!—gave Sergeant McBride (and his demon incarnation) a life of his own.

Levon Hatlo

His first name was taken from the late, great Levon Helm. Levon needed to be "regular army." Upstanding, faithful, and maybe just a tiny bit jealous.

Bloody Bob Karch

In the scripts, this character was modeled on one of Quantrill's Raiders, "Bloody" Bill Anderson, but as Anderson was young and fairly handsome, we wanted something else for Karch. Older, craggier, and frankly a lot nastier looking. He is, after all, needed for one of the key mis-directions in the arc. Those are scalps he's holding in his left hand there.

Captain Thesham

His name was still in development at this point, but Valerio nailed the look of the character pretty quickly. Captain Thesham's Raiders are modeled on William Quantrill's black flag Confederate guerillas. His moustache looks a lot like Quantrill's but we needed Thesham to be a bit more handsome.

Gabby/Gabby Demon

Ostensibly Gabby had to be the least formidable of Thesham's crew. I at first thought of him as looking like the 20th C. character actor, Gabby Hayes. Fortunately for everybody, Valerio didn't take me too literally and we got this much more balanced look for the character.

Here's the first take on the Demon version of Gabby. There's certainly nothing wrong with it. It's hideous, and initially that's the way we were going to go, however...

Major Demons

When Valerio was coming up with the three "major" demons for issue #3, he sent this group drawing to me. When I saw that guy on the right, the goat-demon, I told Valerio "Screw the other Gabby-Demon, THIS is our boy!"

Other Demons

As for the other demons, or monsters, or what have you, Valerio went absolutely nuts. We talked about the right vibe to go for (should they look more like animals, or just monsters? Insect men, or classical hooved devils?) but in the end the only way it was going to work was if it was completely unhinged so Valerio just let his imagination run wild.